When the Corn is Red

When the

Corn is Red

retold by Pekay Shor

with pictures by Gary Von Ilg

ABINGDON PRESS   Nashville and New York

Copyright © 1973 by Abingdon Press
All rights reserved

Library of Congress Cataloging in Publication Data

Shor, Pekay.
 When the corn is red.

 SUMMARY: This Tuscaroran Indian legend explains the
significance of red corn to their tribe and the reason
they lost their land to the white man.
 1. Tuscarora Indians—Legends. [1. Tuscarora
Indians—Legends. 2. Indians of North America—Legends]
I. Von Ilg, Gary, 1938-   illus. II. Title.
E99.T9S53   398.2   72-5129
ISBN 0-687-45094-2

Manufactured by the Parthenon Press at Nashville, Tennessee, United States of America

For Nathan and Nina Starr

"Provide thyself a teacher; be quit of doubt."
—Rabban Gamaliel, *Ethics of the Fathers*

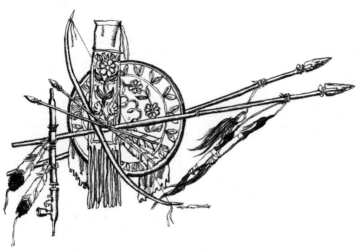

To understand a people one must turn to the myths they have created. Their legends, epics, festivals, songs, and dance-rituals must be surveyed, for it is these that mirror a nation's soul.

Dr. Theodor Gaster, in his comparative study of Sir James Frazer's *Folklore in the Old Testament,* points out that one of the most striking characteristics of myth is that ultimately it finds expression in poetry. Dr. Gaster's work *Myth, Legend, and Custom in the Old Testament* makes clear that the first concern of myth is with experience, and from there it proceeds to the business of translating the *real into the ideal.*

By such means, then, through myth, legend, and poetry, men have from earliest times tried to explain the inexplicable, to fathom the mysteries of nature, to express in simple terms that which has been universally experienced—life in its recurring cycle of birth and death, sorrow, grief, pain, wonder, and joy.

Among the many deprived minorities in our midst, the American
Indian has been perhaps the most tragic and least-understood segment of
our population. Differing in name and local custom, their tribes scattered
across the American continent, the Indians were bound together once—and still are—by a
common thread of humanity. This proud race, out of its anonymous
past, has created a mythology of haunting poignancy, with a simplicity indelibly
and unmistakably its own.

The Tuscarora legend told here was discovered quite by chance in the
musty archives of Augustus Watters' *The Vale of Ramapo*. His reference to
it consists of no more than a brief paragraph. Only one of this author's
friends from the Ramapo region near the New Jersey-New York border had heard it, and his
recollection of it could add little to the material found in Watters.

The badly decimated remnant of the Tuscarora, who became
eventually the sixth nation of the Iroquois, trekked northward from the
Carolinas after several encounters with encroaching white settlers. Many
of the mountain people living in the Ramapos today claim to be descended
from the Tuscarora and are fiercely proud of their Indian blood.

The legend of the red corn is a tale which this author felt
had to be told—and in truth, it told itself. Writing it involved
merely setting down what the inner ear dictated, no more, no less. It is
the author's hope that this legend will be read by people everywhere, but
especially by American Indians, whose self-image will surely one day translate
itself from the real to the ideal, and thus compensate them for the heavy
dues which the long memory of misery has exacted.

PEKAY SHOR

In the days of long ago the Tuscaroras roamed
freely on the land. They fished in the sparkling waters
and, in the woodlands rich with game, they hunted.

One day the Great Spirit called to them and said:

My children, take this gift.
In love do I bestow it
And in love shall you receive it.
It will feed you and sustain you.
It will prosper you and keep you.
Through this gift of corn I bring,
All your children will be blessed.
Only live in peace and friendship,
Live in friendship with each other.

The Tuscaroras were pleased with the Great Spirit's gift.
It was pleasant to the taste and beautiful to look at.
It grew plentifully in tall, slender stalks. It had silken
tassels, and its color, like the color of the
Tuscaroras, was red. For a long time the Tuscaroras were
happy with the Great Spirit's gift. And just as the
Great Spirit had promised, it fed the people
and sustained them.

    But they grew restless and began to quarrel. They
quarreled among themselves and fought with their brothers.
No longer were the Tuscaroras content. They had forgotten
the Great Spirit's words, *live peaceably together!*
Their quarrels were so loud that the noise reached the sky.
The Great Spirit's ears rang with the sound of it.
He summoned the Tuscaroras and spoke words of kindness.

My children, have you forgotten?
Have you forgotten what I told you?
Have you tired of my gift?
Tell me how my gift has failed you,
Why you quarrel, why you fight?
   Heed my counsel, my dear children,
   Rid yourselves of endless discord.
   Make an end of bitter fights.
   Love each other, live in peace.

The Tuscaroras heard the Great Spirit's plea,
but they did not obey. They fought and quarreled until
the noise reached heaven. Again the Great Spirit
called his children and with a sorrowful voice spoke.

I have heard your dreadful quarrels,
And I weary of your wars.
Will you let the jaws of evil
Open wide to swallow you?
Cruel times will be upon you;
All your days will be as nights.
Heed my warning, hear my words,
Lest eternal night befall you.
Learn contentment, study peace.

Still the Tuscaroras would not listen and they quarreled more than ever. When the Great Spirit saw that the Tuscarora would not listen, he turned sorrowfully away.

The evil ways of his children saddened him and his silence
continued for many moons. The stars looked down
upon the quarreling Tuscaroras and wept, the moon turned
pale, and the clouds drifted mournfully away.

At last the Great Spirit could bear it no longer. He
summoned his children once again. He spoke softly and
in sorrow. He spoke of the future, of the days to come.

From a far-off place will come
Strangers pale of face, and fair.
Their canoes are many-numbered;
Tall and stately on the waters
You will see them glide like birds.
When at first you shall behold them,
They will bring you many gifts,
Gifts of wonder that will please you,
Will delight you and deceive you.
For their gifts foreshadow doom.

They will take away your lands,
Take your rivers and your streams;
Take your hunting-grounds and forests;
Take your summer and your spring;
Leave you winter, leave you grief;
Leave misfortune, bring you woe.

As the Tuscaroras listened, they became downcast.

The Great Spirit told them that the coming of the pale-faced
strangers would be marked by an unmistakable sign.
For at that time the gift of red corn which he had given them
would turn white. When the corn became white
the strangers from beyond the waters would inhabit
the land for ten thousand years.

When the Tuscaroras heard this, they wept so that their
tears watered the earth. But the Great Spirit comforted
his people. He told them that they would live through
many sorrows and hardships but a day would come
when the pale strangers would depart. The red man would
return, he would come back to regain his lands.
And he would return in peace.

"How shall we know when that time is near?"
asked the Tuscaroras. The Great Spirit answered.

There will be a sign from heaven
To foretell that far-off time.
There will be a time of waters,
There will be a time of rains,
And the gift of corn I gave you
Shall be seen as once it was.
White no more will be the color.
It will turn again to red,
Like the children of my people,
Burnished, handsome, bright the color!

When the corn is red, my people,
You will come in joy and gladness.

You will come with songs and laughter.
You will come again in peace.